Council Fire

by Elizabet
Illustrated by G

MONDO

In memory of my mom, Vera Sullivan, who loved
both children and reading

Contents

Native-American Names and Their Meanings

Achak [A-chack]: spirit

Aranck [ah-RONGK]: stars

Hiawatha [hī-UH-woth-UH]: he who makes rivers

Jikonhsaseh [jeh-kohn-sah-sey]: known as the "Mother of Nations"

Kajika [kah-JEE-kuh]: walks without sound

Kohana [koh-HAHN-uh]: swift

Mato [mah-TOH]: brave

Oota Dabun [oo-TAH dah-BUHN]: day star

Tadodaho [tah-doh-DAH-ho]: chief

Wematin [wem-AH-tin]: brother

Chapter 1

The Raid
Kohana

My eyes snapped open. Something was wrong. Small hairs rose along the back of my neck, and my heart began to race. I rubbed the last bits of sleep from my eyes and kicked off thick layers of bearskin blankets. Sitting up, I looked across the dimly lit long-house and could just make out my mother's face. She put a finger to her lips, stopping my question before I asked it.

Dawn crept slowly through the longhouse. Soft rays of sunshine poured through the smoke holes in the roof, sending columns of light into the smoky chamber. A shadowy figure came toward me. Slowly I recognized Mato, my uncle. I reached out and grabbed his hand. "What is it? What's wrong?"

"It's a raid," Mato whispered. "Mohawk warriors lie in wait just outside the palisade. Take your position."

As his quiet message made its way through the longhouse, I watched men grab weapons from the storage hooks above the platforms. Shivers ran down the lengths of my arms and back. I couldn't remember a time without this fear, without this blood-shed. Even though I already had ten summers, I wasn't allowed to fight with the men of our Onondaga village. During a raid I had to

5

stay in the longhouse. Last summer I had helped the men build a palisade, a fence of protection, around the village. If the attackers battled their way through the palisade, my cousin, Kajika, and I would stand ready to defend our family.

Quickly I grabbed my bow and arrows. As I walked toward the doorway, a familiar voice behind me barked, "Get out of the way!" Before I had time to react, I was shoved against one of the sleeping platforms. I knew not to complain. The man who had pushed me was my father, Chief Tadodaho. His harsh temper had long ruled our village. I had learned to stay out of his way.

Hurrying to the doorway, I pulled the deerskin flap aside to watch the men of my village gathering silently near the entrance to the palisade. Tadodaho stood in the center of the group, his head covered with great piles of twisted hair that curled round and round like long, ugly snakes. With great effort he lifted his deformed arms and placed his hands on either side of his mouth. In a shrill voice, he yelled, "Wahee! Wahee!"

The warriors moved as one and ran out to meet the raiding enemy. I could no longer see the men. Loud whoops and war cries reached my ears. I pictured the arrows flying between the two groups of men, and warriors on both sides falling to the ground. My eyes yearned to see what my ears could hear. Why shouldn't I join the battle? Why shouldn't I send my arrows flying at the intruders who had come to steal and harm? I felt a longing so strong that my mouth filled with the taste of it. I knew that I should stay at my post in the longhouse, but my feet began to move in the direction of the battle.

Kajika grabbed my arm and cried, "Where are you going?"

I pushed him away. "I'm going out there with the men. I can help them. I know I can. You stay here."

"You're going to get in trouble! You're supposed to stay here, too. Tadodaho will find out that you left. Then you'll really get it. Besides, you hate the fighting."

"Yeah, I do hate it. I wish there was another way besides fighting to prove that I really am brave. But I can't just stand here when men from our village might be getting hurt out there." I shrugged my shoulders and left the longhouse. The women were too busy with the children to notice my leaving. As I got closer to the gate, the cries and yells of the raid became louder. I reached over my shoulder and took an arrow from the quiver strapped to my back. I placed the shaft in the bow and pulled the string back, ready to shoot. Creeping quietly, I moved through the maze that led to the entrance of the palisade. Finally I reached the grassy field. Everywhere I looked, men from my village were fighting with men from the Mohawk Nation.

I tried to aim my arrow at one of the invaders. Everyone was moving too fast. I wasn't able to get a clear shot. I scanned the field, looking for my father, but I couldn't see him. Arrows flew back and

forth across the meadow. A few of the men lay crumpled on the grass, their days as warriors over. And there was Mato! Just as I spotted him, he shoved a Mohawk warrior named Wematin and sent him crashing to the ground. Mato reached for his tomahawk, but before he could use it, Wematin picked himself up off the ground and started to run away. As he ran, he called to the other Mohawk warriors to follow him. All over the field, men pulled themselves away from the battle and ran into the forest.

I was so intent on watching the retreat that I lost my grip on my bow, and the arrow fell to the ground. Just as I pulled a second arrow from my quiver, an enormous arm encircled my chest, and a hand was slapped over my mouth. I was lifted roughly off my feet and wrenched back into the village. I beat on the arm that held me with my fists. My dangling feet kicked at the man who had captured me. But he didn't even flinch. Desperate, I lowered my head and clamped my teeth down as hard as I could, biting his arm.

"Yowwwwch," he howled and flung me into the dirt, knocking the breath out of me. I sat on the dusty, hard-packed earth trying to suck in some air and looked up at the man towering over me. This was no stranger! Mato stood over me scowling, his fists clenched at his sides.

He used a voice so quiet and deadly that I wished that he were yelling. "How many times have you been told not to leave your post? Wait till your father hears about this! What do you have to say for yourself?"

Ashamed that I had not stayed at my post, I couldn't look at my uncle. I knew that no excuse would be accepted. I picked myself up off the ground and stood in front of him, hoping for a forgiveness that did not come. "Go back to your position right now!"

I turned and walked quickly toward our longhouse. When I looked back, Mato had already rejoined the other men outside the palisade. I kept watch from the doorway of our home, knowing that the men would stay outside to make sure that the enemy had really left.

It wasn't long before I heard the loud cheers of the warriors. They had been successful in keeping the raiders away—this time. But the enemy would return to raid again. Then the men of my village would respond by forming a raiding party. They would travel to the land of the Mohawk and raid their villages. They would steal food and tools, just as the Mohawk had stolen from us. This was the way of life for my people. This was the way it had been for all of my time on Mother Earth.

I walked slowly to my sleeping platform and returned my bow and arrows to their storage places. Slumped on the platform, I watched my toes trace lines in the dirt floor. The village would be safe now for a few days, until the next raid came.

The women waited nervously for the men to return to the

longhouse. As each man walked in, he was greeted with affection and warm words of thanksgiving. The wounded were carried to their platforms and tended to by their wives. Small children flung themselves at their fathers and uncles. The warriors were wrapped in warm, grateful hugs of homecoming. Older children stood close behind their younger siblings, also needing to touch and welcome home the brave men.

I didn't join in this celebration of courage and life. I had disappointed my uncle by leaving my post. These were hard thoughts to carry. I knew that I would have to prove to my uncle and to my father that I was capable of better deeds.

When Tadodaho came back into the longhouse, he walked past me without speaking, without even looking at me. He returned his tools of war to their storage places. Normal sounds of morning filled our home as the people readied themselves for the new day.

When Tadodaho walked back through the longhouse, he stopped directly in front of me and roughly grabbed my wrist. "I'm ashamed of you. You left your post and proved to me once again that you are not ready to be a warrior. I keep waiting for you to act like the son of a chief, but it just isn't happening! Maybe someday a dream quest will bring you to manhood, but I'm not holding out much hope for that."

He dropped my wrist, as if touching me burned his skin, shook his head, and walked out of the longhouse.

I worked hard throughout the rest of the day, completing all of my chores. First I slung two deerskin pouches over my shoulder and walked the well-worn path toward the river. Massive trees lined the way, their heavy branches creating a leafy canopy over my head. The rising sun threw slanting lines of light through the trees. Leaves of red and gold showered down on me, blowing across the path, their brittleness crunching under my feet. I walked past stands of brilliant red sumac. The air felt cool against my chest, cooler than it had been even one sun ago. When I reached the river, I knelt at its edge and filled each pouch. I laid them on the riverbank and crouched motionlessly, watching the swiftly moving current. I slowly raised my arm, held my breath, and plunged my hand into the water, lifting out a large bass.

After I had caught three more fish, I headed back to add the catch to the cook pot. Leaving the forest, I walked up a gentle hill to higher ground. An open, rolling meadow stretched out toward the palisade that circled around my village, providing protection against the frequent raids. The long meadow was decorated with the last of the wildflowers. I walked through low-growing bushes of dogbane. Butterflies flew up out of the long grasses with each of my steps.

After I had cleaned the fish, I added them to the soup pot that hung over one of the fireplaces. Using a broad wooden paddle, I picked up a stone from under the pot that had been heated by the fire. I dropped this stone into the pot, adding its heat to the soup. I spent the rest of the afternoon working on arrowheads, carefully chipping away at the stones to sharpen their points.

Sadness still sat with me at the end of the day as I rested on the ground outside of our longhouse. My mother, Oota Dabun, was seated on a thick stump nearby. Her black hair was decorated with combs that had been carved into the shape of birds in flight. As I watched her, she lifted a long cylinder of carved maple wood and, with even strength, delivered it into a hollowed-out wooden base of black oak, crushing the corn held in its basin. The rhythmic sound of pestle beating against mortar echoed throughout the village as she ground corn for the soup pot. The music of her mortar joined with the rhythm of other corn grinders around the village in a thudding song of thanks to the Great Spirit.

When the sun was just two hands measure from the earth, Grandmother came and sat next to me. She said, "A foolish man makes a mistake and does nothing. A wise man makes a mistake and learns all he can from it. You're very wise, Kohana. Soon you'll have enough summers to fight alongside the men. Be patient. Your time is coming."

For the first time that day, I smiled. Grandmother's forgiveness cradled me, and once again I felt included in the life of our village.

Chapter 2

Kajika

A few days after the raid, I sat on my platform to eat my midday meal and made several trips back and forth to the cooking pot for more stew. I watched Kohana's mother as she carefully embroidered porcupine quills on a pair of moccasins. When my stomach was full, I said, "How come you're so quiet, Oota Dabun? I'm used to hearing you sing or talk while you work."

"Oh, Kajika. I'm worried about your Grandmother. She's very sick. I'm sure she has a fever. The sun has been up for a long time, but she's still sleeping. Today is the third day she has slept through."

"That's not good. She is getting pretty old. Do you think she's dying?"

Before she could answer me, the deerskin flap of the longhouse was thrown roughly aside. Kohana burst into the longhouse. He leapt onto the platform just beyond me and shouted, "We have to rake the stones out of the field so the men can play Guh-chee-gwuh-ai! If they play a good game, the Great Spirit might heal Grandmother. Come on, Kajika! Come with me! Get your hoe! Let's go!"

Kohana reached above his sleeping platform and grabbed a long stick that hung from a hook on the wall. Moose antlers had been lashed to one end of it.

I stood on my own platform and grabbed another hoe. Shouting in excitement, we jumped off the platforms and ran down the long center aisle of the longhouse. As we neared Grandmother's sleeping platform, Kohana stopped to speak to her.

"Grandmother, the men are going to play a ballgame for you!" Her eyes didn't open; she didn't even stir in her deep sleep. Kohana gently kissed her forehead and we left the longhouse.

As we raced to the wide meadow just outside the palisade, we were joined by many other boys and girls headed in the same direction, each armed with a hoe. A narrow stream—a stem of the great river—ran close to the field.

We spread out across the field, hoeing the long grasses and looking for rocks that might trip up the players or hurt their bare feet. As each rock was found, we carried it out of the field and threw it into the woods beyond. I worked close by Kohana and quietly asked him, "Do you think there will be a raid today?"

"No, it's too late in the day. We're safe now. I'm sure of it."

"Do you ever get sick of it? Sick of the raids?" I asked.

Kohana stopped hoeing and turned to face me. "Yeah, I do. I wish there was a way that it could always be this peaceful. Father says that men prove their bravery by becoming warriors. But

I think there has to be another way to show our courage. What good does it do to kill and steal from each other?"

I shook my head. "Yeah, I don't get it either. But we better not let anyone hear us talking this way. They'll think we're cowards. Even Mato believes that all that fighting is a good thing."

We turned back to our hoeing job. Young and old began to crowd the edges of the playing field. Blankets were spread out in the shade of tall trees. Families sat together to watch the game. Dozens of men, wearing breechcloths, gathered at either end of the field. Women placed garters of beads and shells around the players' wrists and ankles. Men, now too old to play, painted symbols on the players' arms and faces. Red dye, the color of combat, was used to draw patterns on their skin. I wished that I could stand there with them, to play ball for Grandmother.

People turned to watch as Chief Tadodaho limped slowly toward the center of the field. Kohana took a step backward, probably so that his father couldn't see him. I was pretty sure he didn't want to be yelled at again. When Tadodaho—this man who never smiled, who never laughed—reached the center, a great silence came over the crowd. He raised his horribly twisted arms above his head. His voice rumbled across the field. "Today we play for the Creator. It will please Him to see His children use their strength and power as they play this game of our ancestors. We will see who can throw the farthest and who can run the fastest. We are grateful to play on this fine ground, near this mighty river. Play with honor. Win with honor. Na ho."

The two groups of men formed straight lines across each end of the field. They stood facing each other, ready for the challenge. Each player carried a long wooden game stick. Before anyone else had a chance, I ran into the center of the field and handed a leather ball to Tadodaho. The chief dropped the ball at his feet. The crowd quieted again, anticipating the start of the game.

One man from each of the teams ran forward, stopping just before they reached the chief. Tadodaho held his crippled arms out, pointing his forefingers. He held the two men arm's width apart. The men braced themselves, ready to run. Each player held his stick out directly in front of him. Tadodaho picked up the ball from the ground and held it high in the air. He yelled, "Tah-satawhen!" Then he threw the ball into the air.

Mato was the taller of the two players, and he caught the ball. Cradling it in the net of his stick, he began to run. Players moved in from both ends of the field. Mato was quickly surrounded by dozens of men, each trying to wrestle the ball away from him. One man ran away from the others and yelled, "Here, send the ball here! Over here!"

Mato struggled to lift his stick above his head. He ran backward for several steps. Swiftly turning the stick in his hands to keep the ball balanced in the net, he swung his stick over his shoulder and launched the ball into the air. It flew high and far. One of his team-mates caught it.

The man who caught the ball ran as fast as he could toward the goal tree. Seven or eight men raced after him, carrying their sticks out in front of them. The ball was tossed back and forth between the two men leading the chase. The teams roamed all over the countryside. Everyone who was watching ran right along with the game, yelling, cheering, and shouting directions at the players.

After a long hard run, Mato caught up to the men on his team. As the ball was passed back to him, he lifted his stick into the air at an angle. When the ball hit his net, it dropped to the ground. He scooped the ball up and threw it over his head. With men coming at him from every side, he swung his stick and hit the ball as hard as he could. The ball flew straight through the air and smacked hard against the goal tree.

All over the field, people either celebrated or shouted in anger. Kohana beat me to it. He ran onto the field, scooped up the ball, and brought it back to the center so that the action could begin again. He ran off the field without even looking at Tadodaho.

The game continued throughout the day. Players left the game to rest and drink from the stream and then joined in again. A lot of men were injured, but that didn't stop them from playing. Men who got seriously hurt were simply hauled off the field by their families.

When the game was tied at four goals each, shadows began to creep across the playing field. Soon there wouldn't be enough light to play. Mato once again caught the beginning toss and began to race toward the goal tree. He ran swiftly, turning and twisting his stick to balance the ball. He was so focused on not dropping the ball that he didn't see the huge man running straight at him. *Thwaaaaaaack!* The sound of the collision resonated across the entire field. Mato was knocked flat on his back. He lost grip of his stick, and the ball dropped. Some guy on the other team scooped it up and ran off with it, balancing it in his net. Mato was still lying on his back, gasping for air. He looked over at Kohana and me and motioned for us to come over to him.

Kohana looked at me, shrugged his shoulders, ran to Mato's side, and asked, "Do you want some water? Do you need help walking off the field?"

In a shaky voice, Mato said, "Take my place, son. Run with the men. Hit the goal tree. Please the Great Spirit."

Kohana gently laid the palm of his hand on Mato's face, grabbed his stick, and began to run. I could see the wind blowing through his hair. I could hear the strong rhythm of his legs as he pounded down the field. I was happy for my friend, but I wished Mato had asked me to stand in for him.

Most of the players had surrounded the man who had control of the ball. But not Kohana. He ran on ahead toward the goal tree. His running became smooth and swift like water flowing in the river. As he neared the goal tree, he looked back over his shoulder and called to the other men, "Throw it now! Throw it to me! Now!"

At first it seemed that the men would ignore his cries. But he didn't give up. He kept running. "Look at me!" he yelled even louder. "Throw it!"

Finally the man who had the ball struggled free from the gaggle of men surrounding him just long enough to pull his stick back and let it fling forward. The ball rose up and moved forward, flying with the currents of Father Wind. Still Kohana ran, looking back over his shoulder every few steps. The ball arced and slowly came spinning down out of the sky. Kohana held his stick in front of him, tipping the net up over his head.

With just a short distance to the tree, he spun around and neatly caught the ball in the net of Mato's stick. Whirling back around, he whipped the ball out of the net. He stood there and followed its path with his eyes as it sped toward the tree. I held my breath and waited, a wait that seemed to take forever. Then, with the most joyous splat, the ball hit the goal tree, soundly, in the middle of its trunk. People jumped to their feet and cheered. And suddenly it no longer mattered which team Kohana played for. We all knew that we were watching the birth of a new player, a player with great speed and accuracy.

We raced to Kohana and surrounded him with words of praise and affection. "That was amazing!" I exclaimed.

He looked down the length of the field, and I knew who he was looking for. There, being helped up by another man, I saw Mato raise his hand in tribute, and Kohana returned the salute. Tadodaho walked past Kohana without looking at him, without speaking to him. I couldn't believe that even now he wasn't going to acknowledge Kohana. The celebratory roar of the people was quieted only by the voice of our chief.

"This game ends now with the setting of the sun. The men have played well and with honor. Go now to your homes. Night comes."

Kohana and I walked toward the village alongside the men, our heads held high. He shouldered his uncle's stick and said, "The Creator had to love that game! He has to heal Grandmother after that."

I threw my arm around his shoulders. "I hope so."

The setting sun bathed the western face of each tree in a soft reddish hue. The trees seemed to lean toward the light to catch the last bit of the day's warmth. The sky, in answer to the glory of the trees, raised a band of dusky rose from its lowest edge.

The people walked back through the palisade and began to gather in an open area at the center of the village. We helped pile firewood into a large heap. Soon flames leapt high into the streaked sky, throwing orange and yellow light across the faces of the men who danced around the fire. Women roasted corn and brought the cooked ears to their families. People celebrated the strength of a new player, and a game well played.

When Kohana and I could no longer keep our eyes open, we left the fire and walked to our longhouse. As we neared our home, Oota Dabun ran toward us calling, "Come! Come quickly! It's your Grandmother!"

We ran, my heart beating rapidly. Had she died? What if I never heard the gentle sound of her voice again? I didn't want to go to her side, and yet I couldn't turn away. Oota Dabun reached first for my hand and then for Kohana's. Together we ran toward Grandmother's platform.

We knelt at her side and looked at her beautiful, peaceful face. Her eyes were closed, her hands still. I remembered all of the gentle actions of those hands. I bowed my head as tears began to slide down my cheeks. Kohana's face was wet with tears, too. Oota Dabun lifted our chins gently with her hands and said, "Look carefully, boys. She's getting better."

Slowly Grandmother opened her eyes. Her voice was so low that we needed to lean in close to be able to hear her. "Kohana, I heard that you played well today. I heard that your feet flew across the field, like the great geese fly across Father Sky. You have inherited the strength and speed of your grandfather. He was a mighty player."

Kohana wiped his tears away with the back of his hand. "Grandmother, I'm so glad that you're awake and feeling better! For that, I would run my fastest all day and all night."

"I am glad to be back with you, my grandsons. Kohana, while I was sleeping I dreamt that you were running, and the whole village was watching you. Kajika was cheering for you. This dream tells me that you have important work to do, Kohana. Someday soon our people will call on you to do a great thing. You must get ready."

We stayed at Grandmother's side for a long time. Oota Dabun fed her corn soup and tea made from the bark of maple. Kohana and I warmed her hands.

Later, when we lay on our sleeping platforms deep within the bearskins, Kohana asked me, "What great task could lie before me? Am I really as strong as Grandmother believes I am?"

I answered him. "If she says you are, then you must be."

Chapter 3

Hiawatha

Peacemaker and I had been paddling silently downriver since before dawn. We had long since fallen into an easy rhythm, our paddles matched stroke for stroke. I spent the time thinking about all the villages that he and I had already visited. During our talks with them, chiefs from the nations of the Seneca, the Cayuga, the Oneida, and the Mohawk had decided to join together in a powerful league of nations. After Peacemaker explained his plan to me, I knew that I would do whatever it took to help him carry it out. He thinks that if the five nations stop raiding each other and start working together, we can become a more powerful people. We were on our way to the Onondaga Village where we hoped to convince Chief Tadodaho to bring his people into the league.

We rounded a bend, and—just up ahead—I saw a boy stretched out on a large outcropping of rock that loomed over the river. Above him the branches swayed back and forth, showing little patches of blue sky. The sound of the crickets chirping busily in the nearby bushes and the bullfrogs' deep echo from the cattails nearby were hypnotic. He looked half asleep.

I asked Peacemaker, "Do you see the young man up ahead?"

He stopped paddling and scanned the riverbank. "Yes, I do. Let's see if he knows Tadodaho."

"Hello!" I hollered. "Hello!" The boy was startled and jumped to his feet. Putting one hand to his forehead to shade his eyes from the sunshine, he looked in the direction of our canoe. Standing silently on the rock, he watched as we paddled closer to him. It was then that I recognized him as Kohana, son of Chief Tadodaho.

Kohana moved down the rock to the river's edge. When he finally recognized me, he held up his hand high in greeting. As our canoe reached the shore, he bent low and pulled it up onto the riverbank. We set our paddles in the canoe, climbed out, and stood next to him.

Smiling at Kohana, I introduced him to Peacemaker. "This is Kohana, the son of Chief Tadodaho. For many seasons now, I have watched him grow tall and strong. Soon he'll be old enough to go hunting with his father and the other men." I pointed at my fellow traveler. "Kohana, this is my friend, Peacemaker. He and I are on a special mission. For too long we have seen our people raid each other's villages. We think we have a plan that will stop the fighting. We've been traveling to the other nations in the East and those in the West to talk about the great power that comes with peace. We've traveled here today so that your people may also hear this great message."

Peacemaker nodded and spoke with a low, gravelly voice. "I am very pleased to meet you, Kohana. I know that the Great Spirit will be with us as we carry this message of peace. I also know that your father might not listen to us. It will take many powerful words to change the mind of a great warrior like Tadodaho."

Kohana nodded. "That's for sure. My father is not the least bit interested in hearing about peace. I'm pretty sure he won't listen to you." He looked carefully around us before he continued. "But I'm very interested in stopping the raids. I don't want to see anyone else killed. Everyone is afraid of my father, so we'll have to be careful. If anyone hears us talking about peace, we can get in a lot of trouble. Come on. I'll show you the way to our longhouse."

I put my arm around Kohana's shoulders. "Even if your father won't listen to us, we have to try to spread the Peacemaker's message of peace."

Kohana led the way through the forest. As we walked, a flock of geese flew overhead, winging their way to warmer air. Kohana explained to us about his grandmother's dream. We stood still and watched the geese's progress until they were out of sight.

When we reached Tadodaho's longhouse, Oota Dabun greeted us and handed us bowls of food. We accepted the stew and cornbread with thanks and sat on one of the platforms to eat.

Chief Tadodaho sat on a platform across from us. He held a

large wooden bowl in his lap and was noisily slurping up great spoonfuls of food. The stew dribbled from his spoon and splashed across his chest, dripping down over his large belly. He didn't seem to notice the mess as he hurried the food to his mouth. Kohana's mother kept her eye on Tadodaho's bowl, making sure it did not go empty.

Kohana waited. I think he was especially afraid to interrupt his father while he was eating. Finally he began in a small voice. "Father? You already know Hiawatha. This is his friend, Peacemaker. They have something important to tell you."

Kohana kept his eyes on the dirt floor, perhaps not wanting to see the expression on his father's face.

Tadodaho didn't even look up from his stew. He grunted and continued to shovel food into his mouth. I understood that by staying silent he was showing his disapproval of us. With a small smile and nod for Kohana, I turned to Chief Tadodaho and began to speak. "We're trying to make peace between the five nations of the Iroquois. Peacemaker has asked me to help him spread his message of peace. It brings me great honor to bring you his words.

"The people of the longhouse now live in five separate but great nations: Seneca, Cayuga, Onondaga, Oneida, and Mohawk. These nations have long fought over hunting lands, water, and food. Peacemaker and I hope to bring an end to all that fighting.

We want the nations to agree to live in peace. By joining together as brothers, we will be an even stronger people who can live in harmony here on Mother Earth."

Tadodaho continued to eat his stew, ignoring us. Peacemaker cleared his throat and said, "The nations of the Mohawk, the Oneida, the Cayuga, and the Seneca have already agreed to this plan of peace. Their chiefs think it is a good plan. We ask you, Chief Tadodaho, to bring your people, the great nation of the Onondaga, into the League of Nations."

Tadodaho slammed down his bowl. Jumping up, he moved quickly across the center aisle of the longhouse until he stood directly in front of Peacemaker. He jabbed his forefinger at Peacemaker and shouted, "What will this stupid plan of yours do for me? We don't want to be brothers with the other nations. Onondaga men have always fought for hunting lands and waterways. We don't need your help. We don't want your help. Get out of my longhouse and get out of my village. Take your foolish message of peace with you."

Kohana and I looked at each other. I was sure that he wanted the fighting and the raids to stop as much as I did. He swallowed hard and said, "Father, I have listened to this message of peace. If you talk to our people about it, I think they'll want to be a part of it, too."

Chief Tadodaho whipped around and stared at his son. His eyes held no love and no warmth. He looked back at Peacemaker and at me. "Now see what you've done? Your words are coming out of my son's mouth. You and your message aren't welcome here. Don't fill my son's mind with any more of this peace talk. The son of a chief is a warrior. He will stand tall with his brothers and fight against any threat. No more words, no more talk of peace. Get out!"

Tadodaho returned to his platform, picked up his bowl, and started slurping his stew again. I signaled to Peacemaker and Kohana, and the three of us left the longhouse together. We walked side by side through the village without speaking. All around us the Onondaga people were completing their daily chores. The rhythm of life in any village usually sang in my heart, but that day I heard no music. Our dream of peace would come true only if Tadodaho would listen. But he had not listened. He had been much more interested in what was in his soup bowl than what was in Peacemaker's heart.

Kohana looked up at me. "I'm so sorry. It's never a good idea to talk to my father while he's eating."

Peacemaker walked with his head held high, a small smile upon his face. "Don't give up, my friends," he said. "I'm sure that eventually our message will be heard. We'll wait for three suns to pass. Then we'll try again to speak to Chief Tadodaho."

"You will?" asked Kohana. "You'll try again? I'm so glad to hear you say that. But where will you stay while you're waiting? You can't sleep in my longhouse. You won't be welcome there, that's for sure."

He was silent for a few minutes as we kept walking. "Oh, wait, I think I know of a place. It's near our village. While you're waiting, I'll have time to talk with my mother and my grandmother. The raids have filled their hearts with fear, too. I know they'll listen to your plan."

"Whose house are you taking us to?" I asked.

"Jikonhsaseh's. She lives in a small house by herself. Her husband died a long time ago. She lets warriors from all the different nations stay in her home. She feeds them and nurses their wounds. I know she'll welcome us. You can stay with her until it's time to try talking to my father again."

I stopped walking. "I don't know if we can trust Jikonhsaseh. I've met her before. I'm not so sure that a woman who feeds warriors will want to hear about a plan for peace."

Peacemaker put his hand on my shoulder, and we continued walking. "Don't worry. I've met Jikonhsaseh, too. When I first came upon her home near the waterfall, she welcomed me, thinking that I, too, was a warrior. She gave me food and shelter. I watched as she cared for the other men, getting them ready to return to the raids and violence of this war between brothers. When the men were gone, I spoke to her about the plan for peace. Her ears were opened and the good words touched her heart.

Take me to Jikonhsaseh's home, Kohana. We'll rest and talk and wait. We'll pray that Tadodaho's ears will also be opened, so he may come to know and want the plan for peace."

Chapter 4

Kohana

I led the men as we walked single file through the cool damp forest. We didn't speak but moved quickly along. The narrow path we walked followed a ridge high above the valley. Below us the river pulsed forward, its water tumbling and dancing in the fading sunlight.

Thoughts and questions swirled through my mind. *Should I help these men? If I do, I stand against my own father. But my heart tells me that peace is the right way. I trust Hiawatha. He's a good man. I see wisdom and kindness when I look into Peacemaker's eyes. What would Grandmother say if she knew that I held council against my father?* After walking a long time, I answered my own question. *I think Grandmother would tell me to follow my heart.*

As we walked along, I felt that someone or something was following us. I hadn't seen anyone, but the hair on the back of my neck stood up. I could hear the sound of my heart thumping in my chest. Standing still, I listened intently for a sound—a stick breaking or the scrape of a branch—but I heard nothing. I didn't express my fears to Peacemaker or Hiawatha.

The sun had long left the sky by the time we reached Jikonhsaseh's home. A broom or stick propped against her door would be a sign that she was not at home. Jikonhsaseh's door held neither. I called out, "Jikonhsaseh, you have visitors."

She appeared in her doorway and looked at us. "Welcome back, Peacemaker. You've brought my good friends Hiawatha and Kohana. Welcome to my home. Come in. I will give you food and water."

Hiawatha and Peacemaker walked into the small house. I turned and took one last look through the mingling shadows of the forest before I entered her home. Once inside, she served us succotash and cornbread. I was hungry from the long walk and grateful for the food. Before we ate, we gave thanks to the Great Spirit for the food and friendship.

After we had eaten, Jikonhsaseh cleared the wooden bowls away. Then Hiawatha asked her, "Is it true what Peacemaker told us? Have you had a change of heart?"

"Yes, Hiawatha. It's true. Peacemaker showed me that by feeding the warriors, I was helping the hatred and the fear to grow. Without even realizing it, I was helping the raids to continue. Now my heart is open, and my mind is clear. I now know that if we all learn to live in peace, we will be a stronger and happier people. I no longer feed or tend to the warriors."

"Thank you, Jikonhsaseh," Peacemaker said. "We talked to Tadodaho, but he wouldn't listen. If it's all right with you, we'll stay here for three days. Then we'll try again to bring our powerful message to the Onondaga."

Jikonhsaseh smiled. "You're welcome in my home for as long as you need to stay."

While Peacemaker, Hiawatha, and Jikonhsaseh talked, I sat quietly, close to the doorway. I continued to listen for noises from outside. I couldn't shake the feeling that someone had been following us. I still felt danger was close by. I didn't want anyone to hurt my new friends. Slowly, without their noticing, I moved toward the doorway and slipped out.

I bent low, keeping my body pulled in and close to the ground. The moon spilled light between the trees, allowing me to find the path. I moved quietly and slowly, scanning the woods for any sign of movement, listening for noises of an intruder. I pulled my knife from the sheath that I carried around my neck. I held the handle firmly, pointing the blade out in front of me.

I heard no noise but sensed that whatever was out there was somehow now right behind me. I held my breath and whirled around to face the danger.

A huge form sprang at me from behind a thick elm tree. I pulled my arm back, ready to plunge my knife into the shadowy mass. But before I could react, a man's huge hand grabbed my wrist as tightly as one of my snare traps. The knife dropped out of my hand. He spun me around, lifted me off of my feet, and wedged me tightly against his chest. His other hand covered my mouth.

I tried to scream but couldn't make a sound. I tried to open my mouth to bite, but he held me too securely. My kidnapper dragged me off into the woods away from the warmth and safety of Jikonhsaseh's home. I wondered if my friends even knew I was gone. I kicked and squirmed, but he wouldn't let me go.

Now he began to run. My teeth jarred together with each pounding step, my body still imprisoned by my captor's strong grasp. I tried twisting around to see the face of this cruel man, but I was held too tightly and couldn't move. He carried me into the night, farther and farther away from Jikonhsaseh's home. Finally I gave up and stopped struggling. My body became limp. As the strange journey continued, I even dozed a little. Each time I woke, my fear was renewed. Where was this man taking me? What would happen to me?

Just as the first streaks of dawn spun across the sky, I was set down on my feet. I came fully awake. I was surprised when I looked up only to once again find the face of my uncle. "Mato, why did you take me away from my friends?"

"Those people are not your friends. They talk with empty words. Warriors talk with action. The men of our village have always protected the people. You know that your father doesn't want this plan of peace, and he's the chief. He is so mad at you for siding with these people."

I nodded. "I'm sorry that you and Father are angry with me. I knew that you would be. But Peacemaker believes that strength and power will come from these good words of peace. He says that this is what the Great Spirit wants. I know that I should listen to my father and follow his words. But Peacemaker's words are so much stronger. We could stop the raids, Mato. The people would stop fighting with each other. They would stop hurting each other. How can a plan that stops the death of warriors be bad?"

Mato looked away from me. "It isn't for me to decide these things. I'm not a chief. Your father's word must be obeyed. I brought you here so that you could have some time alone to listen to your own spirit. You must build a shelter for yourself and search for a dream vision. Maybe then you will know the true path to take."

I smiled and nodded my head. "I love you, uncle. I will build a shelter and search for a vision. I promise you that I'll search my heart for the truth."

Mato stood and looked at me for a long time. It must have been hard for him to kidnap me. I thought it would be even harder for him to leave me here alone. He turned and walked away from me. I watched him leave, staring at the spot where he had exited the forest long after he had left. I knew that I could try to find my way back to the warmth of Jikonhsaseh's home. I even took a few steps in that direction, but then I sat down. Closing my eyes, I thanked the Great Spirit for bringing me to this important quest.

After a while I began to focus on the sounds around me. I could hear a trickle of water and knew that Mato had made sure that I would not be thirsty. Birdsong floated to me along with the scurrying noises made by tiny paws in search of food. The forest would provide for me. But first I would need a shelter.

I found that my knife had been returned to its sheath. On the ground near my feet, I found a tomahawk, a bow, and arrows. My uncle had left the tools that I would need. I began to cut narrow branches from the willow trees all around me. A pile began to grow. Soon I had enough to begin building. Clumps of dogbane grew nearby. I cut several stalks of the plant and sat down against the trunk of a huge oak tree. Pulling the casing off the plant, I pulled the stringy fibers apart. Holding three fibers in one hand, I rolled them against my thigh with my other hand, as I had watched my mother do many times. Soon I had a fine piece of twine. I repeated this process over and over until I had made a small ball of twine.

I used the blade of the tomahawk to dig several small holes in the ground, set in a circular pattern. I trimmed the end of each branch into a sharp point and then shoved each branch into one of the small holes. After the branches were secure, I bent the branches toward each other, tying them together with the fiber twine. When all of the branches were in place, I went in search of birch bark to lay over the structure.

Finally the shelter was complete. I crawled into the small structure and lay down. I listened to the wind and the water, to the animals in search of food, to the birdsong. Soon my eyes closed, and I slept.

Later I awakened slowly. I looked out of my shelter and saw that the sun was very low in the sky. The first threads of dusk crept toward me. Hunger called to me, but I didn't listen. I crawled out of my shelter and stood up, listening for the sound of moving water. I walked toward that sound until I came upon a small stream. I scooped up water in my hands and drank until my thirst was gone. Red streaks filled the sky as I walked back to my shelter. Lying down again, I listened to the sounds of the forest, waiting for sleep and hoping for a vision.

Sleep came again—full of dreams that danced so quickly behind my eyelids that I was unable to hold onto them. Grandmother spoke to me, but I couldn't hear her words. The image of her face faded. It was replaced by the angry face of my father. Smoke from several fires drifted across the faces in my dream. Soft light poured in, pushing out the smoke. The light dimmed, leaving a dark blue blanket. One by one stars appeared in the blanket. I recognized the familiar night sky. Slowly I felt myself being pulled up until I was there in my own dream floating high in that night sky. I wasn't flying but was somehow balanced and safe watching the stars dance around me.

Although they weren't with me, I felt the love of my mother and my grandmother. Their love wrapped around me like one of my thick bearskins. I could hear Peacemaker's words. I could see Hiawatha's kind eyes.

I turned to see Jikonhsaseh, who appeared to be floating beside me. She beckoned to me, and I moved closer to hear her words. "Listen carefully to me, Kohana. The moon will be your guide. Follow the moon's light."

I looked for the moon but couldn't see it. I turned back to Jikonhsaseh to ask for help, but she was gone. Her words were still swirling around me, "Follow the moon's light."

Stars danced around me, moving closer and closer together. One cluster of stars spun into another, their light growing brighter. And there before me, hanging in the deep blue night, was the moon—full, round, and glowing. Floating still, I didn't find it strange that I should be so close to the moon. I was so glad that I couldn't stop looking at it.

Geese flew silently across the face of the moon. Shards of moonlight danced off their strong wing feathers. The moon seemed to travel with the birds, continually shedding its soft light on their journey. The birds began to sing. At first I couldn't hear the words, but as more geese appeared, the song became louder. The words became clear. I watched and listened for a long time, until I could sing the song of the geese. My voice joined with theirs in a song that echoed among the stars.

"We move with strength,

We move with purpose,

We move as one.

Each in support of the other,

Each in support of the other."

My heart was flooded with great happiness. I knew the name of this invisible and powerful life force: *Orenda*.

Finally, when the sun was already high in the sky, I woke from my long dream. I gathered my belongings and began to look for a way back to my village. I decided to follow the river's path until the land became familiar.

My dream had come. My vision quest was complete. I now knew what I was meant to do.

Chapter 5

Tadodaho

Mato and I worked together, replacing some of the elm-bark shingles that had fallen off the roof of the longhouse. The new bark, soaked flat in the stream, would keep the longhouse warmer during the coming months of snow. This was not an easy task for a man whose arms were so misshapen. However, I refused to give in to my deformity. Years ago I would have been the man on top of the house putting the bark in place. Now I could only stand on the ground and pass the bark up to Mato.

I passed him another piece, and he said, "I've been watching Kohana ever since he returned from his quest. I would love to know what happened up there. He seems to be happier. Has he said anything to you?"

I shook my head. "No, nothing."

Mato set the piece in line. "Well, he really can't tell us anything until the Midwinter Festival. Still I can't help wondering."

I scoffed. "I don't hold out much hope for him. He's always talking about how we should get along with other people. He doesn't say those things in front of me anymore, but I know he is talking to other people around the village. That just makes him sound weak.

If my son is not a warrior, I don't want anything to do with him."

Mato was silent for a while. When he spoke, his voice was quiet. "He's a good boy, Tadodaho. Almost a man. I don't see any weakness in him."

I turned my head sharply toward him. "Not you, too. First Hiawatha and Peacemaker fill my son's head with all their yammering about peace, and now you're going soft on me, too? There is no room in this village for any man who is not willing to go to war against our enemies."

Mato didn't respond.

We spent most of the day repairing the roof. When the shadows lengthened, and we could no longer see our work, we went inside the longhouse, hungry for a meal. Oota Dabun served us soup. After I tasted it, I threw my spoon down and said, "This needs more meat in it. It tastes weak, like that son of yours."

My wife did not answer me. But Kohana stood up from his platform and faced me.

"Speak your thoughts to me, Father. I'm right here."

I looked at my son and laughed. "Oh, so now you're going to be brave? Your new friends have managed to get the other nations to end the raids, so there's no chance of you having to prove yourself as a warrior. It's easy to be brave when there's no enemy."

"Are you my enemy, Father?" Kohana took a step toward me. His voice was quiet but firm. "Do you hate me?"

Oota Dabun tried to step in front of Kohana to protect him from me. "No, Mother," he said. "I must face him on my own."

She looked at me—her eyes filled with tears—then moved back away from him.

"Do you hate me, Father?" he repeated.

The other people in the longhouse had grown quiet and were looking at me. A chief must always look powerful in front of his people. "You aren't worth any of my time. Why should I bother hating someone who won't stand beside me? Go find your weak friends and bother them. Look around you, Kohana. This village is filled with men who are brave enough to fight beside me in battle." I crossed the distance between us, put my hand on my son's chest, and pushed him down on the platform, out of my way. Oota Dabun did not look at me as I walked past her. Nor did any of the other people. I left the longhouse and walked out of the palisade into the silent woods beyond.

I turned at a noise behind me and found my mother following me. She smiled at me and took both of my hands in hers. Although I tried to pull away from her, she held me firmly in her grasp. She said, "Tadodaho, your anger has grown tiresome. You strut around this village barking orders at everyone. You rule from a position of fear, my son. That is not the model that your father provided for you. I have watched you push your son out of your life, and he doesn't deserve it. You are a mean and spiteful man. Where does all of this anger come from?"

I pulled my hands away from her. "You, too, Mother? You, too? If you don't like the way I run things around here, why don't you try living with the Seneca? I'm sure they would be happy to have you."

I turned my back on her and kept walking into the forest. When I reached the river, I picked up small stones from the bank and threw them as hard as I could into the water. My arms ached from the effort. They hurt every minute of every day. I was tired of living in constant pain. Each new season they seemed to become more twisted, more useless. No one must find out that my arms have gotten worse. What kind of a chief would I be if I couldn't hold my bow or my tomahawk?

The forest—alive with the sounds of animal life—calmed me. I sat down on the bank of the river. I thought of Kohana and the expression on his face as he fell back from the force of my shove. I shook my head and shouted at the trees, "I am the chief. They will listen to me. I will take my men, and we will find food for the winter. We will fight against our enemies. Ever since Hiawatha and Peacemaker first came here, my family hasn't treated me right. No more! I am the chief!" My words rattled around in the empty branches above. Piles of leaves were strewn about the riverbank, as faded and colorless as my heart.

I heaved myself up from the riverbank and returned to the village. "Mato! Mato! Where are you?"

I finally found him carrying baskets of squash into the underground storage pit. "Tell the men that we will be leaving tomorrow. The soup is weak; our supply of meat must be restored. If we leave now, we should be able to find enough game to sustain us through the winter and still be back in time for the festival."

Mato finished unloading the squash and turned to face me. "And what about Kohana and Kajika? Shall I tell them, too? Will you allow them to hunt with us?"

My face darkened. "Absolutely not. There will be no weak-kneed boys on this trip. The warriors of the Onondaga will provide for this village as we have always done."

Chapter 6

Kajika

$\mathcal{S}$tark mounds of snow covered the village. Smoke poured from the roof hatches of the longhouses, sending lazy white trails across the pale blue sky. Several moons had passed. The snow had brought a great stillness that wound its way around the bleak landscape. Most of the birds had migrated to warmer homes. Plants and animals slept. The people waited for the promise of nature—the rebirth of all living things.

Inside the longhouses, little kids played with cornhusk dolls and miniature tools. Men repaired tools, chipped away at arrowheads, and talked. Women tended the cooking pots or made baskets and clothing. The wood was piled high on the fires to ward off the deep cold. Wrapped around everything were the smells of sweet grass, soup, soot, bear grease, and tobacco. Everyone in the longhouse knew that the time inside would be long. Words from the storyteller and music from the musicians filled the time. Patience and kindness were expected. The parents and the elders practiced both so that the young could learn.

Hiawatha and Peacemaker had come back three different times to try to talk with Tadodaho. Each time he had turned down their plan of peace. "I don't need your foolish plan of peace," he had said. "Look around you at my strong warriors. We don't need your help. Go away!" Hiawatha and Peacemaker were saddened but were strong in knowing that they could not give up.

Kohana had long since returned from his vision quest. He carried the message of that night deep in his heart. Even though I kept bugging him about it, he wouldn't tell me anything. It would soon be time for the Midwinter Festival. Then he would have to share his dream with our village. While we waited for the festival, we began each day by bringing water to the longhouse. Every morning Kohana and I pulled heavy bearskins over our heads. Mother had sewn two large pelts together, leaving a hole just large enough to slip my head through. We wore the fur side of the skin on the inside to warm our bodies. We also pulled on sleeves made of bearskin. A long piece of fibrous twine ran over our shoulders, connecting the sleeves. We rubbed bear grease into our cheeks, lips, and forehead to keep our skin from chapping.

Just before we left the longhouse, we took snowshoes from the storage area near the entranceway. We slid our feet under wide leather straps that were attached to a hickory frame.

Leaving the village, we climbed over the great white hills, our snowshoes keeping us from sinking into the snow. Gone was the deep green of the forest, leaving only black branches and pine trees against a brittle blue sky. The cold air snatched away my breath

and hurt the skin on my face and hands. We hurried to the river, trying to keep the warmth of the longhouse in mind.

"Hey, Kohana! Did I tell you I saw the Dancing Sister Stars?"

"You did? Were they really low in the sky?"

"Yeah, they were right on the horizon."

He scooped up handfuls of snow and threw them at me. "Great! That means the men will come back from their hunt, and the Midwinter Festival can begin! I can't wait for the hunters to come back. Think of all that juicy meat they'll bring with them! Yum!"

When we reached the river, I used my tomahawk to chop a hole in the ice that had formed on the surface of the water. As quickly as Kohana could, he lowered the vessels into the hole, filled them, and tossed them to me. Throwing the water satchels over our shoulders, we turned and hurried back through the forest toward the open meadow. The hills of snow and ice made travel slow and hard. The harsh wind blew at us, and we leaned our bodies into it, pushing our snowshoes forward, one after the other.

As we neared the palisade, a distant noise scared me. I started to ask Kohana if he thought it was a raid, but then a wide smile replaced my fear. "Whew! At first I thought it was a raid. But warriors wouldn't come this late in the day, and they wouldn't make so much noise in their coming. It's got to be the hunters returning!"

We stood just on the fringe of the forest, waiting for the men to appear on the horizon. I was so excited that I forgot how cold I was.

Kohana turned to me and said, "I think this will be the last time that we'll have to stay behind in the village when the hunters leave."

"Me, too. They have to let us go next time. We've grown taller just since they've been gone."

Men began to walk out from a break in the tree line. Tadodaho came first, followed by dozens of other men. Their noise drew people out of the village to greet the hunters. The little kids came first, running to greet their fathers, brothers, and uncles.

Then the women came, many of them pulling empty wooden sleds across the wind-swept snowbanks. The sleds would be used to carry the meat home to be smoked and stored. The men had left their catch at the edge of the forest. If the men brought the meat in, anyone in the village could claim some of it, and no one could be turned away. If the wives brought the game in, they would not have to share it. Once the meat was cooked, all who came to the door would be offered food.

Mato walked over and hugged both of us. "Hello, nephews. I'm very glad to see you. The hunt was successful. You can see we've brought home a lot of meat. The cooking pots will be full until Mother Earth wakes again. Tonight we'll eat, dance, and give thanks to the Creator."

"Welcome home, Mato," I said. "I'm glad to see you, too. The longhouse has seemed empty without you in it. And my stomach sure is glad for the meat you've brought!"

The people worked together to put away the tools and the game from the hunt. In each longhouse, preparations for the festival were underway. Food stores were brought out from under the sleeping platforms. Dried vegetables were brought down from the storage racks under the arched ceilings of the longhouses. Smells of roasting corn, stew, succotash, soup, and cornbread soon filled the air. The village was preparing for the renewal celebration of midwinter: *Ganah'owi.* The festival would begin with the sunrise and would last for seven days.

I had trouble falling asleep. When I looked over at Kohana, he, too, lay on his cornhusk mat and waited restlessly for the celebration. When dawn finally came, everyone dressed carefully, wearing necklaces of bone and copper. Two of the elders, dressed in shaggy buffalo robes, entered the longhouse. Their heads were decorated with braided wreaths of cornhusks. Braided cornhusks were wound around their ankles and arms. The old men stirred the ashes in the fires until all of the flames were extinguished. They placed some of the ashes in each corner of the longhouse.

"Now you must clean your house and rekindle a new fire," said one of the elders. "Don't think about the troubles of the past. That time is over. Clean your heart and forgive your enemies. May the Great Spirit bring the people of this household seasons of health, happiness, and well-being." The elders left the longhouse.

When the cooking fires had been rekindled, Kohana and I went to the main longhouse to join with all of the other families.

Tadodaho stood near the fire in the center of the longhouse and offered the prayer of thanksgiving.

"Great Spirit, listen to all of the people who are gathered together here today. Smoke rises, carrying our thoughts to you."

He took a pinch of tobacco from a small leather pouch and threw it directly on the fire, sending thick clouds of smoke toward the ceiling.

"Kindly listen to the words as they come in the smoke. We thank you for the coming season of planting. We ask for a good season with many crops."

Again he threw a pinch of tobacco on the flames. "We are grateful for the people, for Mother Earth, for the plants, the water, the trees, the animals, and the birds. Keep us healthy and away from sickness. Keep our old people strong and our young people safe. Na ho."

Several men began to play instruments. Some of them used simple wooden sticks to tap out a beat on water drums, while others shook rattles made from turtle shells. Two of the musicians faced each other, straddling a long bench. Each man pounded the edge of his rattle on the bench, the heavy sounds echoing through the longhouse.

The first dance began. I recognized it as the feather dance, performed to thank the trees and bushes. The dancers slowly shuffled in a winding pattern. Kohana and I watched, waiting for the rhythm to increase and the dancers to move faster. Fathers and uncles carried the smallest children as they moved with the ancient rhythms. I joined the dancers. As I circled with the people of our village, I wondered about Kohana's vision quest. Even though I wished that he had told me about it, I was still thankful that he had finally met his spiritual advisor.

When I got tired of dancing, I yelled over to Kohana. "Hey, let's go play snow snake! I think some of the others are already playing." We put our outdoor garments on and went in search of a game of snow snake. We walked toward the meadow and soon heard voices.

"Yes! My stick went farther than yours did! I win!"

Before our last sleep, Mato had helped me prepare a tunnel for the snow snake game. First we had to drag a log for many steps. This left a trough in the snow. We sprinkled water carefully into the trough. That water was now frozen, leaving a slippery path for the snake to follow. The snakes were made of a skinny stretch of hickory wood as long as I am tall. Each snake had a carved head on one end and a tapering tail on the other.

When the boys who were already playing saw us, one of them said, "Oh, great! You're just in time to play on my team. These other guys think that they're going to win, but you two can help me beat them."

"Definitely!" said Kohana. "I'll go first!" He picked up the long snake with his right hand and balanced the end of it with his left. Holding it up above his shoulder he began to run toward the trough. He hurled the snake as hard as he could. It whistled through the air, landed in the trough, and sailed a long way before stopping.

I ran to mark the spot. "That was a good throw! They can't throw that far!"

Both of the boys on the other team wanted to go next. They fought about it for a while. Finally the taller of the two boys won the argument and took his turn. His throw went even farther than Kohana's had.

When it was my turn, I carefully lifted the snake and threw it, but it crashed into the side of the trough and there it stuck. "Well, maybe I'll do better next time."

Our side won a few points, but when the boys on the other side scored seven points, it was time to end the game. Just then Mato's voice rang out across the meadow. "Kohana! Kajika! Come here!"

I looked at Kohana. "Maybe he wants us to help clear the snow from the river, so we can play a ballgame on the ice."

Kohana looked over at Mato and hollered, "We have to go and get our sticks."

"No, you don't! I don't need you for a ballgame. We're going to have a race! You two should run in it!"

We looked at each other and grinned. I said, "We might have

lost the snow-snake game, but there is no way we can lose in a race, not with your feet!"

"We're coming, Uncle!" yelled Kohana.

Chapter 7

Kohana

Men and boys of all sizes and shapes had prepared for the run. Kajika and I joined them in a line that spread across one end of the meadow. We took off as many layers of clothing as the cold would permit. The heat of running would warm us. Soon a large pile of clothing lay at each runner's feet.

What a beautiful day to run! Grandmother Sun shines on us. Soon she will melt the snow, and a new planting season will begin. I will race with Grandmother Sun shining on my shoulders, Grandfather Wind at my back, and the Great Spirit looking down on me.

Mato stood at the other end of the meadow ready to start the race. In his powerful voice, he said, "Great Spirit, we are thankful for these healthy bodies that wish to run for you. These men will run a fair race in hopes that you will smile upon their efforts. Ahsawe!"

The race began.

At first many of the men and boys were ahead of me. They ran very fast. I didn't watch the ones in front of me. I didn't think of the ones behind me. Joy filled me as my body fell into the rhythm of running. Over and over my arms swung up and down. I gave no order to my legs to move, but their motions came swiftly. The movement of my legs and arms was fluid, and—with very little effort—I began to pass other runners. First I passed the men who had as many years as my father. The music of my footsteps brought a smile to my face.

As I passed one of Mato's friends, he said, "Look at Kohana! He's smiling! We huff, puff, sweat, and breathe in little gasps, but Kohana is smiling!"

Now I began to pass the younger men, the same men who had played with me in the great ballgame. Their faces were not happy when I passed them. One man that I passed sped up his steps to match my stride, but soon he tired and fell back.

There were only three men left ahead of me. I had done well. It was enough to be so close to winning. But still my feet kept up the rhythm of the run.

The man just in front of me began to slow down. Suddenly he stopped and grabbed his side. My long strides allowed me to pass him.

Now there were only two men ahead of me. The end of the meadow was in sight. Were there enough steps left to pass the other men? Both of these men were runners for the Onondaga Nation. Whenever Tadodaho sent a message to another village, one of these runners would carry it, running on the many trails that connected the villages of the Iroquois. These men were able to run all day or all night.

My joyful heart carried my feet faster across the icy meadow. I knew only the rhythm of my body and the wonder of the wind against my face. The Freezing Moon had brought deep cold to everything in the forest, but I felt warm and peaceful as I neared the end of the meadow.

I didn't see the people of the village gathered at the finish line. I didn't hear the cheers and cries of my friends and family. Deep within my own rhythm, I heard only my own footsteps and the sound of my heart keeping pace with my running.

All at once I was grabbed roughly around the waist and thrust up into the air, my body flopping back down into the arms of my uncle. "You won! Kohana, you won the race! The Great Spirit smiles down upon you!"

Everyone swarmed around me, cheering and shouting my name. My small runner's smile slowly became the huge grin of a winner. I leaned back against my uncle, and his deerskin tunic warmed my bare skin. Kajika ran up to me, gasping for breath. "Kohana, you ran so fast! I couldn't keep up with you! You won! I can't believe you won!"

I hugged my cousin. "Thank you, Kajika. After all that running, my stomach tells me it's time for the feast to begin. Let's put our clothes back on and go see if the meal is ready."

Kajika, Mato, and I walked together into the largest of the longhouses. We sat on platforms and ate many bowlfuls of the hot meat and corn soup. I looked forward to the last day of the festival when fry bread, squash, beans, and potatoes would also be served.

After the meal was finished, I went back to my own longhouse and lay on my platform, warmly covered by bearskin. Again I felt the wonder and the power of the race. Even as I drifted off to sleep, it still felt as if my feet were flying across the frozen meadow.

The days of the celebration flew by. On the final day of the festival, I woke earlier than usual. My mind was so preoccupied that I couldn't sleep for long. Kajika and I left the longhouse together. The morning was stark and crisp. We joined other men who were walking toward the sweat lodge at the edge of the river. Kajika turned to me and said, "Can you believe they're letting us go in there with them? Finally!"

Outside the sweat lodge a large fire roared. Inside the lodge a hole had been dug directly in the center of the floor. Using long wooden paddles, men brought large hot rocks in from the fire and placed them into the hole. Then they threw water on the rocks to create a humid cloud of steam within the lodge.

I sat in the sweat lodge between Mato and Kajika. I didn't dare look at my cousin. I knew that if I looked at him, I would laugh, and I was trying hard to be a man. I didn't think that men were supposed to laugh in the sweat lodge.

Just when I thought I couldn't stand the heat any longer, Mato stood and began to scoop up large handfuls of sand from the ground. He rubbed and scrubbed the sand all over his body. Kajika and I copied his motions, and soon the three of us were completely covered in streaks of mud. With a sharp cry and a motion from Mato, we followed him and ran from the sweat lodge, down a small hill, and then right into the icy water of the river in a place where the ice had been chopped away.

"Waaoooooooooooooo!" I screamed. My body had gone from the fiery heat of the smokehouse immediately into the frigid cold of the river water. I felt that I had been turned inside out. I knew that this was a ritual I would now experience every day, but I thought it would take some time to get used to the shock of the cold water. I looked at Kajika and started laughing because his eyes were as big as game balls! I said, "Are you breathing, cousin? You should breathe."

Mato lifted Kajika up out of the water and threw him playfully into a deeper part of the stream. He came up out of the water gasping for air.

"Oh, I see that you are breathing now!" Mato said. "Do you need another throw?"

"No, thank you!" Kajika scrambled up onto the shore. We followed him out of the water. Then we ran back to the longhouse for heat and clothing. We joined the other members of our village in the largest longhouse to listen to the prayer of thanksgiving.

After the prayer the dances and games began again. Late in the afternoon, the babies who had been born in the time since the Green Corn Festival were brought forth in front of the people to be named. The oldest woman in each longhouse had the honor of choosing the name from a long list she held in her memory. Each baby was held up to the people, and his or her name was announced.

Finally it was time for Dream Guessing. I listened carefully as other people told the stories of their dreams. Dream tellers acted out their dream while all of the people listened. Men and women took turns guessing the meaning of the dreams.

Grandmother stood in front of the people. "During my long sickness, I had a curious dream. I dreamt that Kohana would become important to the people. I dreamt that all of the people watched and cheered as he ran fast through the soft meadows of the Sky World."

When Grandmother had finished speaking, I walked over and stood by her side.

"Grandmother, I, too, have a story to tell. Back during the Moon of Leaves, Mato took me into the deepest part of the forest and left me. There I stayed for four days. On the last night, my vision came. You and mother were there, Grandmother, but you left.

Then I was alone in the night sky, floating safely among the stars. Jikonhsaseh, the woman who used to feed the warriors, came to me and said, 'Follow the light.' The stars began to swirl, and they showed me a path of light. That spread of cool light pulled me, and I followed it until I found the moon. As I watched, a great flock of geese gathered and flew across the face of the moon. They sang a song as they followed their path to home. Now I ask you and the people for the meaning of this dream."

People all over the longhouse began to discuss my dream. One of the men said, "This is the boy with great speed."

"This boy is the son of Chief Tadodaho," said one woman.

"That does not change the meaning of his dream," another woman pointed out.

Grandmother said, "When we look at your dream, we see speed in the flight of the geese, true path in the spinning stars, and a destination in the face of the moon."

Mato had been very quiet. I knew that he had been listening to everything. Slowly he stood and walked to the center of the longhouse to join us. "The mighty geese always return to us in the Moon of New Growth. Jikonhsaseh told Kohana to follow the light. This is a boy who will run with the light on the path of truth. This is a boy who will carry messages for Chief Tadodaho."

Grandmother said, "My grandson, you are no long Kohana. In the great tradition of our people, I have the honor of renaming you. Now you will be called Aranck."

All around the longhouse, there were murmurs of consent. People repeated the words *truth* and *path* and nodded their agreement. I turned to Mato and hugged him. "Thank you for your wise words."

I turned to Grandmother and hugged her, too. "Thank you, Grandmother, for teaching me to listen."

"I am very proud of you, Aranck. Now tell me. When are you going to take me to meet this woman you call Jikonhsaseh?"

Chapter 8

Grandmother

The Moons of New Growth brought rain and warmth to the fields outside the palisade. Once again women and girls planted the three sisters: corn, beans, and squash. We relied on these three foods to see us through the Moons of Snow. The sun shone warmly, and gentle rains had nourished the tender plants. The women tended the crops, and the men brought home baskets of smoked fish from the river and the lake. Boys and girls picked strawberries.

One morning after my chores were completed, I visited with Aranck. "Today is a good day to travel. Would you like to take me to meet Jikonhsaseh? I want to meet the woman who brought answers to your dream quest."

"It's a long walk, Grandmother. Do you feel well enough?"

I smiled at my grandson. "These feet have been walking for many seasons. They were walking before your feet were on Mother Earth. They were walking before your mother's feet were on Mother Earth. They still have some walking left in them."

"That's great, Grandmother. Let's go then."

We walked single file on the narrow trail. Leafy boughs

overhead gave grateful shade to our travel. Aranck walked first, but he kept a slow pace. I knew that he was worried about tiring me out. Often he stopped to comment on a tree or an animal.

Finally, with a twinkle in my eye, I said, "Thank you for telling me about the animals and the trees, Aranck. Did you think that I did not know these things? Or is it that you think I am old and need to rest?"

He did not stop again.

We walked for a long time. When the sun was directly overhead, I heard the gentle spill of a waterfall. We stopped to drink the clear, cold water from the stream. I recognized that part of the stream and asked if we were close to Jikonhsaseh's home.

"Yes, Grandmother. We are close. I hope that she will welcome us. Do you think she still follows the plan of peace? Or do you think we will find warriors in her home?"

"I trust Peacemaker. Let's finish our journey."

Aranck led me to the front of Jikonhsaseh's home, and then he called, "Jikonhsaseh! I have brought my grandmother to meet you."

She pulled back the deerskin hanging in her doorway. "I am so glad to see you again, Kohana. Welcome, Grandmother. Come in, and I will give you food."

We went into her small home. There was no one else in the house and no evidence that warriors still came there for shelter and food. She served us soup and boiled bread.

She asked Aranck, "Have you seen Hiawatha or Peacemaker?"

Between swallows of soup, he said, "No, I haven't seen them for a long time."

Jikonhsaseh sat on her platform and shook her head. "I haven't seen them either. Has Tadodaho accepted the peace plan?"

"No, they keep trying to talk to him, but he is still not open to the plan."

"The last time that you were here and you disappeared, I was so worried about you. But Peacemaker was sure that you would be safe. Did you find your spiritual advisor?"

I answered her. "My grandson did dream. And you, Jikonhsaseh, came to him. You led him to the moonlight where he saw a flock of geese flying fast through the night. Mato tells us that he will be a runner and carry messages for the chief. Kohana is now called Aranck."

Jikonhsaseh looked at me, a beautiful smile stretching across her face. "Yes, of course, this is the path he was meant to follow. When Peacemaker brought the good words of peace to me, they gave me the power to enter Aranck's dream and lead him to his answers."

"Thank you, Jikonhsaseh." Aranck looked toward me and said, "We're tired after the long walk. Will we be able to stay here with you and go back to our village in the morning?"

Before she could answer, I said, "Aranck spares the feelings of my old feet. I am the one who tires and would be grateful to stay the night."

"Of course you must stay here, and we will talk of many things."

Our words came and went as the sun swept across the sky. Just as the first stars appeared in the sky, we heard footsteps outside the small domed house. It brought a chill to my skin. Before I was able to react, I heard a familiar and welcome voice.

"Jikonhsaseh! Can two weary travelers once again ask for your welcome?"

She quickly jumped up to greet Hiawatha and Peacemaker.

"Why, hello, Kohana!" said Hiawatha as he walked in. "Hello, Grandmother!"

"Since the time of his dream interpretation, this young man is renamed Aranck," I said.

Hiawatha and Peacemaker looked at each other and then at me. They smiled and nodded with approval of the new name. I, again, told the story of his dream quest while Jikonhsaseh brought the men soup and bread. When they had finished eating, they told us of their journey.

"We have been back to the Mohawk, the Oneida, the Cayuga, and the Seneca," said Peacemaker. "Chiefs in all of the villages still agree with the plan of peace. But we can't make it work without Chief Tadodaho. Every time we talk to him, he shouts at us and tells us to leave. We've been searching our hearts for a way to open his mind. All he can talk about is how powerful he and his warriors are."

Over the years I had often heard my son Tadodaho boast. I was used to his ways. "I think what we need to do is think of something to offer him, something that will make him think that he will be even more powerful."

The small room grew quiet. Finally Jikonhsaseh spoke. "What if we told him that he would be in charge of the council meetings? He could be the most noble sachem of all. We could call him 'First Among Equals.' And what if we told him that the meeting would always be held in the land of the Onondaga? You could give him the job of keeping the fire for the council. That might be enough to persuade him."

"Oh, Jikonhsaseh!" said Peacemaker, jumping up and hugging her. "When I first met you, you were a woman who fed and encouraged enemies to keep fighting. But your heart has opened, and you have made a promise to always live in peace. Now you bring ideas to us that might just bring about this great plan. Because of your great heart and wise mind, we will see to it that women will always have an important role in the plan of peace. You, Jikonhsaseh, will always be the symbol of women. You will be called the 'Mother of Nations.'"

Hiawatha nodded his head in agreement. "We'll talk with Tadodaho again and offer your ideas to him. But I think that the chiefs of the other nations need to be there when we talk to him. We want Tadodaho to see the strength of many behind our offer. Runners must be sent with this request to all of the other nations. We'll need runners of great courage and great speed."

Jikonhsaseh and I looked at each other and smiled. We looked at Aranck and smiled again. At first he put his head down and said nothing. No one spoke. There was only the crackle of the fire and the soft hoot of Father Owl resting in a distant tree. Then Aranck raised his head and spoke in a clear, strong voice. "I will be one of the runners who carries the message. My feet will fly along the trail, and I will tell the chiefs to come."

"That is a great decision, Aranck," said Hiawatha. "We will see your dream vision come to life. I will give this same message to other runners so that all of the chiefs will know that we need them."

Peacemaker smiled. "Sleep well, Aranck. Your body must be well rested. You must run to the east and give this message to our Oneida and Mohawk brothers. I am proud of your courage. I know that you will do well."

Working together, we made sleeping places in the small house. Before too long I heard the gentle whiffling snore that Aranck made. His sleeping sounds were soon joined by deeper snores from Peacemaker and Hiawatha. I did not rest well. I lay awake for a long time. The words of Mato came back to me over and over again. "This is a boy who will run with the light on the path of truth." I believed that Aranck had the kind of courage it would take to be a message runner, but I worried for his safety. When sleep finally came, my dreams were filled with strange shapes and noises.

Chapter 9

Aranck

The next morning the sun hadn't yet warmed the earth when I was ready to leave Jikonhsaseh's home. She gave me a leather pouch of cornmeal and maple syrup. Then she wished me well on my journey.

Grandmother smiled at me and hugged me for a long time. "Don't worry about me, Aranck. Hiawatha will see that I find my way home again."

"Tell the chiefs to come to the north shore of the Great Lake that lies near the Onondaga people," Peacemaker told me. "They must come when the geese once again fly south. You must wear this 'talked' wampum belt and show it to the chiefs." He placed a belt that contained a message around my waist, tying it securely. Most of the quahog shells on the belt were purple. In the center of the belt, there was a tree made of white shells connected by lines to two white squares on either side, symbolizing the five nations.

"Aranck," said Hiawatha, "your path is long. You must run first to the east to bring the message to the Oneida and then on to the Mohawk. I will send other runners to the Seneca and the Cayuga. The Great Spirit will be with you."

I didn't speak. I turned and walked toward the path. I stopped and looked back at the faces of the people that I loved. Then I turned once again and began to run.

I settled into the journey and surrendered my body over to the rhythm of running. My eyes took in the still beauty of the great tree trunks that lined my path. I smelled the moist earth under my feet, the wildflowers and grasses that filled the open spaces, and the musky scent that was the life of the forest. A gentle breeze cooled the air, bringing with it birdsong and the chattering of squirrels.

Several times I stopped at small streams to quench my deep thirst and eat from the pouch Jikonhsaseh had given me. So quiet was I that at one stream a deer and her fawn joined me to tend their own thirst. I realized that I was but one small part of Mother Earth. The deer and the water were my brothers.

On and on I ran. My feet were grateful for the soft cushion of old leaves and pine needles on the path. The sun traveled across the sky, warming my shoulders and always throwing its light across my path. Even when the sun had finally left the sky, I didn't stop. I followed the stars and knew that I could trust their direction.

The sun had long since set when I reached the land of the Oneida. I was greeted warmly and brought to a longhouse where I gave Peacemaker's important message to the chiefs. The men listened to the words carefully and agreed to travel to the north shore of Onondaga Lake. They thanked me for bringing them the message.

One of the chiefs brought me to his longhouse and gave me food, water, and a place to rest for the night. This time my sleep came very quickly, and I had no dreams.

Deep in slumber, my nose started to itch. I didn't want to open my eyes. I wiggled my nose and hoped that the pesky fly would leave, but the itch came again and again. When I finally opened my eyes, I didn't find a fly but instead found a small boy staring at me. The boy, who looked as if he had only three summers, held a tiny feather in his hand just a small space from the end of my nose.

"You sleep and sleep and sleep," he said. "Are you sick?"

I looked around, remembering that I was in the land of the Oneida, in the longhouse of the kind and generous chief. The way the light came into the roof hatches told me that the sun was half way through its journey across the sky.

I jumped off the platform, nearly knocking down the small boy who had been tickling my nose. Righting the child and patting him on the head, I moved quickly to the doorway and out into the village. The woman who had fed me was sitting outside the longhouse carefully pressing clay into long coils in readiness for the pot they would become.

"Thank you for your kindness," I said to her. "I have to go now and take the message to the Mohawk."

The old woman nodded her head, brushing the white strands

of hair from her eyes. "May the Great Spirit go with you on your journey and carry you safely to the end of your path."

I left the village quickly and continued my run to bring the message to the Mohawk. This part of my journey would follow the path of a great river as it made its way east. I waited for the rhythm of my legs to begin, but instead I felt pain in each muscle. My body remembered all of the running from the day before and was not ready to run again. By thinking of only the message and the great plan for peace, I was able to start running in spite of how sore my body was.

As I ran east, the sun traveled west, sending a long shadow out in front of me. The shadow grew longer and longer until it merged with the dark. Then the light from the sun was gone. Still I ran. I ran past great trees that held families of opossums and owls. Branches of pine trees seemed to reach out in front of me, making my passage more difficult. I stumbled over a gnarled tree root and fell hard on the ground, scraping the skin on my knees and hands. It took a long time for me to stand. But still I ran on, lifting each heavy foot in front of the other. Lifting each tired arm to keep pace, on I ran.

Tears came to my eyes. Steps came slower; I could not catch my breath. Sobs came from my throat as I felt failure creeping up on me. I fell to my knees on the path, unable to make my feet take another step. I didn't think that I would be able to complete the journey. My shoulders shook as I cried out my anger and sadness. "Why have I been given this job? I am not man enough for it. Fear floods my heart now, and my body is too tired to finish this run."

The forest closed in around me. I felt so terribly small and alone. My friends were counting on me, and my body had failed me. I lay down on the dirt path and wept. My tears ran down over my cheeks and into the hard-packed dirt of the trail.

I stayed that way for a long time. Finally my breath came more slowly. I looked at the powerful trees on either side of the path and wished for their strength. I had to keep going. How could I return to my village now? A man did not give up. I looked up at the trees, asking the Great Spirit for strength to finish my journey. The moon still shone down upon me. I was grateful for the friendship of this moon. It gave its light freely and lifted my heavy heart.

Suddenly, silently, a few geese flew across the face of the moon. They stayed in its light, winging their way home. More geese joined them, their silhouettes outlined by the moonlight. Slowly my body filled with new energy, and I stood up straight and tall on the path.

"Thank you, Great Spirit, for giving me strength. I know that you are here with me and that you will travel with me every step of this journey. My feet will run now knowing that you are here to guide them on this important path. Thank you, Great Spirit."

Slowly, one small step after another, I began to run. I remembered the words that Jikonhsaseh had taught me, and quietly I began to sing:

"We move with strength,

We move with purpose.

We move as one.

Each in support of the other,

Each in support of the other."

Chapter 10

Wematin, Mohawk Chief

I led the line of warriors along the narrow path, pushing stray branches out of our way. As we approached a wide bend in the trail, my brother, Achak, caught up to me and said, "Are you sure this raid on the Oneida is the right thing to do?"

I shook my head and answered, "I really don't know. I was so sure that the Peacemaker's plan would work. Joining our nations together made sense to me. But it has been months now that we have waited for word about Tadodaho. You know that our warriors miss the taste of battle. I couldn't keep them at home in our village any longer."

The shadows were lengthening. I knew that we would need to stop soon and rest for the night.

I raised my hand to signal the other men behind me to stop. As I did, I heard a noise ahead of us on the trail. I signaled for silence. It was a slapping sound, the kind of sound made by bare feet running along a hard-packed trail. Because of the curve in the path, we were unable to tell who was coming.

Achak and I exchanged glances. He said, "It sounds like there is only one person running." Again I used the signal to silence the men. We waited, the sounds on the path getting louder and louder. Suddenly coming around the bend there appeared a young man, his eyes so intent on the trail that he still had not seen that his path was blocked. He was almost to us before he realized we were there. It took no effort for Achak and me to catch hold of his arms and capture him.

He saw the war paint on our faces. His eyes filled with tears. With his head down, he said quietly, "I have failed them."

Achak shook him and yelled, "Who are you? What is your business here?"

I could feel the men behind me stirring, moving forward, wanting to take out their frustrations on this one young man. Again I held up my hand. The men quieted, and I said to them, "This is not a raiding party. It is just one boy."

One of the men yelled, "Let's kill him and send his scalp as a message to the other nations that the Mohawk way of life will rule."

The other men cheered and pressed forward on the path. Two of the men grabbed the boy and knocked him to the ground.

Another man yelled, "We can kidnap him. Turn him into a brave Mohawk." Again this statement was met with wild cheering from the men.

It was then that I noticed the wampum belt he wore. "Who gave you that?"

Tears still streamed down his face. He looked up at me and whispered, "Peacemaker. Peacemaker talked the belt and gave it to me to bring to you."

"You know me?" I asked. He nodded.

I held my hand out to him. He grabbed it and pulled himself up off the ground. "You are Wematin. You know Mato, my uncle."

I recognized the name Mato—a man I had met many times in battle. "Where is Mato now?"

The boy was having trouble catching his breath. "He's at home now. He will be waiting at the Great Lake in the Onondaga Nation. All of the chiefs will be there waiting."

Achak laughed. "You're telling me that Peacemaker finally got Tadodaho to go along with the plan?"

I waited for the young man to answer. He looked at us, his face washed in sadness.

"No," he said. "We still haven't convinced my father to agree to the plan. But Peacemaker wants all the chiefs to come to the lake when the geese fly south and offer Tadodaho the jobs of keeping the fire and holding the council meetings. Peacemaker thinks if everybody shows up, he might finally agree to it. It was Jikonhsaseh's idea."

The man right behind me shouted to the others, "Hey, we've got Tadodaho's kid!" He lifted the boy up into the air, and a huge roar rose up from the crowd of warriors. Achak wrestled the boy back down and out of the man's strong hold. I stretched out my hand toward the boy and motioned for him to give me the belt.

He untied it from his waist and handed it to me. Achak and I squatted and laid the belt out on the trail. Tracing the first white square with my finger, I followed the path to the next square and then to the tree in the center. Then my brother traced the white lines with his finger. Achak and I looked at each other.

Achak said, "I think he's telling the truth. This tree in the center—I think it symbolizes the job they are offering to Tadodaho. His nation is in the center of the Iroquois land."

The boy shook his head in agreement. "That's the Tree of Peace. It will stand as a symbol of our unity."

I traced the last square on the belt—the one that stood for our Mohawk Nation.

"What are we waiting for?" yelled one of the warriors. "I thought we were going to send Tadodaho a message? Come on, let's kill the boy!" With one swift movement, he pulled his knife out and stepped toward Tadodaho's son.

I stood in his path. "Put the knife away. Violence is no longer the answer. We have received the message we have been waiting for."

The warrior didn't put his knife away. He stood there, so much taller than I, waving the knife back and forth in front of my face. I grabbed his wrist, knowing that he was stronger. "Don't ruin this chance for us. Look at the belt, and you will see the message for

yourself. Let's go to the council on the Great Lake. If the belt is wrong, if Tadodaho isn't convinced, then you can kill the boy."

He still held the knife out in front of him, but he looked at the belt that was spread out on the ground. Looking first at Achak, then at the boy, and finally at me, he said, "I will wait." He put the knife back into its sheath and turned back into the crowd of warriors.

I turned to the young runner and asked, "What is your name, son?"

"Aranck."

"Well, Aranck. Return to your people. Tell Peacemaker that when the geese fly south, we will be waiting for him on the shore of the Great Lake."

Chapter 11

Peacemaker

I watched Aranck as he sat on a log near the water's edge. He chipped pieces off of a large stick and tossed them one by one into the Great Lake, watching the ripples made by the splash. A glorious forest bordered the lake. The leaves of the great maples were a brilliant red. Neighboring trees were dressed in oranges and yellows. The thick grasses had grown as high as his knees. Squirrels and chipmunks scrambled to bury small stores of nuts near their nests. The sun took less and less time to make its arched path across the sky. The people of the many villages had worked hard to tend and then harvest the fields. The longhouses and underground pits were filled with great stores of food for the coming moons of snow.

During the last few days, chiefs from all four nations had been arriving at this place. Earlier, when the sun's first rays had streaked the sky, Aranck had helped many other boys drag large logs into a clearing. Several men dug a hole and put dried sticks and tinder down. Over that they built a tent of fallen limbs and logs. As the sun rose up from the pine-skirted lake, the fire was lit, and people began to gather around it.

Great sparks flew up from the many logs that burned. I looked through the smoky haze at the faces of the people around the fire. The chiefs had come.

Aranck came to stand beside me and said, "My heart is full with the knowledge that I helped bring these important men to this place."

"Yes, Aranck, from the Cayuga, the Seneca, the Mohawk, and the Oneida, the chiefs have come. Here around this fire, warriors who once faced each other in battle now sit shoulder to shoulder. Men who had known no other way of life than that of warfare have come to make peace."

"But there are many more people here than there are chiefs. Who are all of the others?"

"Many people followed their chiefs to hear the plan of peace."

Aranck nodded. In the midst of all the talking and greeting that was going on around the fire, Jikonhsaseh began to sing. She sang of the good words and the power that would come when all of the nations lived in harmony with the gifts the Creator had provided for all. Her voice was soon joined by the music of many drums and rattles. Her words rose with the smoke from the fire and encircled all who had come to hear. Slowly, with just a word here and there, the chiefs and the people joined with Jikonhsaseh and sang the words of peace: "Hail! Hail! Hail! Hail! Hail! To the Great Peace we bring greeting."

At the end of the song, I stood on a wide tree stump and said to the people, "Thank you for coming to be a part of this great plan. We must find a way to bring these good words to Chief Tadodaho. Without the people of the Onondaga Nation, our plan will not work. Chief Tadodaho remains strong against this idea of peace. Jikonsaseh, Mother of Nations, tells us to offer Tadodaho the job of tending the council fire here in the land of the Onondaga. He will be the most noble sachem, the First Among Equals. He will send the messages in talked wampum and call together the council to meet here on the shores of the Great Lake." All around the fire, chiefs from the different nations nodded in agreement. "Let's go find Chief Tadodaho and make this offer to him."

The people stood and walked behind me along a path close to the shoreline. Young women bent forward under the weight of cradleboards strapped to their backs. Small children ran around the edges of the crowd, not yet knowing the importance of this gathering.

We searched a long time for Tadodaho and finally found him in a swampy area. He sat at the foot of a great tree, glowering at us. His hair was so tightly snarled that it stretched the skin on his face. His sad twisted arms sat uselessly at his sides. The crowd of people stood quietly before him. "I can't believe that you're here again with the same words. How many times do I have to tell you? I don't want to hear any more of your noise."

I held my hands out toward him. "We have a new offer for you. If you agree to the plan, your Onondaga people will tend the fire and keep the wampum talked with our messages. You will lead the councils right here in your land. You will send runners when it is time for a council to be called. You will be the most noble of all sachems."

Tadodaho snarled out ugly laughter. "These offers don't change my mind. I don't accept your plan. The Onondaga will not be a part of it."

I did not speak. No words came to me. I searched my heart but just couldn't find another way to try to convince him. Hiawatha didn't speak either. But Jikonhsaseh began to sing. She sang the words of peace. Soon she was joined by all of the chiefs and all of the people. The song grew stronger. Its words floated up out of the swamp, washed over the lake, and mixed with the sunlight in the high arch of the sky. It was strong and rich. It covered the people in deep contentment.

"Your song doesn't change my mind," yelled Tadodaho. "I don't need your peace! Go away and don't ever come back here!"

The strains of music slowly faded from the trees, the water, and the clear blue sky. The people were quiet. Tadodaho was so tortured with hate that his arms were twisted and his hair filled with snakes. In all that misery, he could not hear the beautiful music of the people.

Then one voice began again—strong, deep, and clear. It was the voice of Mato. I was surprised that finally this great warrior had decided to join the quest for peace between the brothers. His song rolled over the swamp and across the glassy surface of the lake. It climbed the great tree trunks and danced across the faces of the changing leaves. The beautiful song floated over the people, filling their hearts once more. Finally it wound its way to Tadodaho, covering him with its beauty and intent. Slowly, ever so slowly, I raised my hands and touched Tadodaho's cruelly bent arms. As I did this, Tadodaho's arms were straightened, the painful twists smoothed out. Jikonhsaseh walked forward and placed a headdress made of deer antlers on Tadodaho's head.

As Mato's song continued to fill the forest and the lakeshore, Hiawatha went to Tadodaho and combed the snakes from his hair, leaving it long and dark and shiny. The great chief, now rid of his hatred and his misery, began to weep quiet tears. He felt the welcome of all of the people. He stood up to join them. Onondaga chiefs came forward and joined the chiefs from the other four nations.

"Please follow me to a great tree—the Tree of Peace," I said. "I have so much to tell you."

I reached out a hand toward Tadodaho. He took it in his own. The people followed behind him. When we reached a tall white pine tree near the shore and near the great fire, I said, "Honored chiefs, form a circle around this great tree. Hold hands to make the circle strong. If we stand united, this tree will always stand. If we let go, the circle will be broken, and the great tree will fall to the ground, breaking the peace."

The chiefs made a circle around the tree, and the people stood behind them.

"We thank the Great Spirit for bringing us here today to stand in the presence of this great tree. The roots of this tree stretch out in the four sacred directions across the land, to the north, the south, the west, and the east. Today we will decide the words of the Great Law of Peace: *Gayanashagowa*. All those who accept the plan of peace will always find shelter under the Tree of Peace. It is so tall that it can be seen from distant places. During the Moons of Snow, New Growth, and Falling Leaves, throughout the seasons for generations to come, this tree will stay green. Just as the tree stays green, so will the Great Peace forever exist among the five nations." I turned to face Aranck and said, "Bring me one arrow from each of the great nations."

Aranck walked around the inside of the circle of chiefs, taking one arrow from each nation. He carried the five arrows and held them out to me. But I did not take the arrows. Instead I drew one arrow from my own quiver.

I said, "Watch how easily this arrow breaks." I held the arrow at either end and easily broke it in two. "Now hand me that bundle."

Aranck handed the arrows to me, and I tried to break them with my hands. I could not do it. I tried to break the five arrows across my knee, but the bundle would not break. I held the unbroken arrows up high for all to see. "When the five nations bind together, they are so strong that the peace cannot be broken. It is only when a nation leaves the whole, that the peace will be broken. We now combine our individual powers into one great power."

I laid the arrows, still bound together, at the base of the Tree of Peace.

"I see peace in the eyes of the people, but I see weapons in their hands. We must bury these weapons of war under this tree, as we promise to never again spill the blood of our brothers." I looked up at the tree. "Grandfather Pine, I ask permission to pull your roots from the ground."

The chiefs came forward, one from each nation, and helped me to uproot the tree. As the great roots were pulled from the ground, a huge hole appeared. One by one the people came forward and dropped their tools of war into the ground. When all of the weapons had been thrown into the hole, the Great Tree was righted.

I looked around the great circle and said, "We cast these weapons of war into the ground. We bury them from sight forever, and plant again this Grandfather Pine. We bury jealousy, hatred, and greed along with the weapons of war. Now the Great Peace is established. Rekindle the fire. Let the smoke from the fire carry these words to the Great Spirit and set our promise to live together under Gayanashagowa, the Great Law of Peace."

Spikes of flame from the great fire licked the sky. Once again the people sang the song of peace. Dancers shuffled their feet and moved in circles around the fire. Musicians added to the beauty of the dance with drums and rattles.

Aranck moved slowly in the circle of dancers with people from all five nations. The heat from the great fire warmed the dancers, but I believe that the knowledge of peace warmed their hearts. Just as Aranck danced close by me, Tadodaho approached him and softly touched his shoulder.

Aranck stepped out of the line of dancers and stood in front of his father. Slowly Tadodaho lifted his arms and placed his hands on Aranck's shoulders. Aranck placed his own hands over those of his father.

Tadodaho said, "My anger and fear have come between us. But Peacemaker's plan has come into my heart, and the anger and fear have left. My ears have been opened; my thoughts are clear. I'm proud of you, Aranck. You have become a strong young man without help from your father. Is there room in your heart for me?"

Aranck smiled. "Of course there is! Does this mean I can hunt with you and the other men?"

Tadodaho returned his smile. "Yes, Aranck. You will be a part of the next hunt. And Kajika can come, too." He put his arm around

Aranck's shoulders, and the two stood together and watched the dancers circle the fire.

I walked toward them. With a hand on each man's shoulder, I waited for the music to end. Then I said to the people, "Should there come a time when problems arise between us, when tempers flare between the people, Tadodaho's runners will call us. We will come to talk and resolve our differences. We shall meet here in this place, by this lake, at this Great Council Fire. All five nations must live together in peace in one Great Longhouse with the sky for a roof and earth for a floor. The Seneca people will be the keepers of the western door, while the Mohawk will keep the eastern door. The Cayuga and the Oneida will be the younger brothers. The great Onondaga people will be the keepers of the fire. We now are united in peace—brothers and sisters under the watchful and loving eye of the Great Spirit."

Dancers wound their way around the fire, moving to the ancient rhythms of drum and rattle. Songs were offered, and the words of peace were lifted up into the sky, floating gently across the lands of the Seneca, the Cayuga, the Onondaga, the Oneida, and the Mohawk.